And Twelve
Chinese Acrobats

For Carolyn
Aida
Rothberg
for fun, for enjoyment
for meeting the Yolens!
Jane Yolen
95

JANE YOLEN

ILLUSTRATED BY **JEAN GRALLEY**

PHILOMEL BOOKS   NEW YORK

And Twelve
Chinese Acrobats

Text copyright © 1995 by Jane Yolen. Illustrations copyright © 1995 by Jean Gralley. Published by Philomel Books, a division of The Putnam & Grosset Group, 200 Madison Avenue, New York, NY 10016. Philomel Books, U.S. Pat. & Tm. Off. All rights reserved. This book, or parts thereof, may not be reproduced in any form without permission in writing from the publisher. Published simultaneously in Canada. Printed in Hong Kong by South China Printing Co. (1988), Ltd. Book design by Nanette Stevenson and Donna Mark. Lettering by David Gatti. The text is set in Palatino.

Library of Congress Cataloging-in-Publication Data Yolen, Jane. And twelve Chinese acrobats / Jane Yolen, Jean Gralley p. cm. Summary: When Wolf's spirited older brother Lou, whom he idolizes, is sent away to military school in Kiev, life is not the same for the Yolen family. [1. Jews—Ukraine—Fiction. 2. Family life—Fiction. 3. Ukraine—Fiction.] I. Gralley, Jean, ill.   II. Title.   III. Title: And 12 Chinese acrobats. PZ7.Y78An 1995   [E]—dc20   93-5355 CIP AC   ISBN 0-399-22691-5
10 9 8 7 6 5 4 3 2 1 First Impression

To the Yolen uncles and aunts, living and dead:
Louis, Eva, Sylvia, Vera, Rose, Sam, Harry
and my father, Will
and to my grandmother, Mina
and my grandfather, Samson,
whom I only knew in stories –JY

For Trina and Rosebud –JG

This is a true story, as true as I can make it. It is about my papa when he was a little boy in Ukraine in 1910. His name was Velvul, which means "Wolf." And he lived with his three brothers and four sisters and his mama and tata in a little village near Kiev called Ykaterinislav.

The house they lived in was large and part of a family compound. Tata was a bottler, a merchant who dealt in oil for lamps, and he was well respected in the village.

Now the house was always full with the bustle of serving girls and Mama in the kitchen. And it was full with the sounds that eight children make. And full with the visits of the village elders, for they always asked Tata's opinions.

1

Whenever anyone came to call, Mama would stand in the door, saying: "Come in, come in. Where there's love, there's room."

And there always was.

Now Wolf loved his four sisters, who fussed over him and tried to comb his yellow curls. He loved Tata who smelled of tobacco and sweat,

and Mama who smelled of powder and borscht. He loved baby Aron who followed him everywhere and Simcha who insisted on being captain of every game.

But most of all he loved his oldest brother, Lyovka, the one they called Lou. Lou the Rascal. Lou the Sinner. Lou the Terrible.

It was Lou who stole raspberry pies from Mama's kitchen and shared them with the peasants in the field. It was Lou who filched ribbons at the fair and brought them home for the serving girls. It was Lou who took lye soap and on Simcha's Torah eve soaped Tata's name on the windows of the butcher shop. It was Lou who smiled when Tata scolded, shaking an angry finger stained brown with tobacco.

And it was only Lou who could make Mama laugh and cry at the same time, ending all his stories with: "And if you will believe me, you will have caviar for breakfast and champagne at each day's end." She would rock with laughter at the stories, till the tears flowed down her red cheeks. Holding her hand over her heart, she would cry: "Stop! Stop! Let me catch my breath, you rascal." At that he would tell her another story, funnier than the first.

It was also Lou who had shown Wolf the greenfinch nests, high up in the oak overlooking the soldiers' trenches.

"Don't say a word, little brother," he had whispered, hoisting Wolf into the tree and then swinging up after him. "If we are very quiet, we will be able to watch the nestlings learn to fly."

But then one of the birds had fallen from the nest and broken its neck. Wolf could not stop sobbing. At last Lou had said, "If you will smile for me again, I will let you play with my tin soldiers."

"Even the general?" asked Wolf.

"As long as you take great care." And that was a special treat because even Simcha was not allowed to touch them.

No wonder Wolf loved Lou best.

*

Now one day when Lou was almost a man,
the village elders came complaining to Tata.
They hammered on the door and when the serving girl opened it, there were seven scowling
men, including the rabbi, waiting angrily outside.
She curtsied and ran to get Tata.

Tata ushered them into the parlor, shutting
the door, but Wolf listened at the keyhole.

"This time," the butcher said, his voice shaking, "he has gone too far."

"He took a cart," said the grocer.

8

"Perhaps he only borrowed it," Tata mused.

"And piled it high with lambs," continued the grocer.

"*Borrowed*," added the butcher, "from different farmers."

"One can borrow lambs," Tata said, "if one means to put them back in the end and no harm done." But his voice was tight and it made Wolf shiver.

"*Pilpul*," said the rabbi, which meant it was a silly argument with words, not real meaning.

9

"And he set the lambs free in the village center," said the carpenter, a very skinny man with a wandering left eye. "This I saw myself."

Tata made a noise through his nose, something like a sneeze and something like a laugh. Wolf put a hand up to his own mouth, afraid he might make the same noise.

"And the lambs got into the mayor's garden and into the village graveyard, and three fell into the soldiers' trenches and one broke its leg there," said the rabbi.

Tata grunted then, and Wolf did not like the sound.

Just then a hand landed on Wolf's shoulder. "What are you doing? I am older than you. I want to hear." It was Simcha, and so Wolf had to let him have the keyhole, though he made a face behind Simcha's back.

The door was opened suddenly and Simcha was caught eavesdropping. He was hauled into the room by his shirt collar by the butcher, who had very big hands.

Wolf burst into laughter, but of course by then the door had been closed again and nobody heard him. But it was the same kind of laughter Mama always made when Lou teased her, part happy and part sad, and Wolf was not sure which part was the greater.

*

After dinner, Mama and Tata stayed up late into the night talking. There was an angry, buzzing sound from the parlor, the sound of them quarreling. And they never quarreled.

"It is too much," Tata said one time. "Never again."

Mama said, "But he's a *good* boy, Tata."

Wolf hated the sounds and put the pillow over his ears.

In the morning Lou was gone.

Gone?" asked the girls plaintively. Even the serving girls, fingering their blue and green ribbons, looked sad.

"Gone?" asked Simcha angrily, because he had not been told before the others and had gotten the spanking that, rightfully, should have belonged to either Wolf or Lou.

"Gone?" wailed baby Aron, not even sure what *gone* meant, but hating the sound of it.

But Wolf knew already that Lou was really and truly gone. The house seemed so much bigger, so much quieter, so much emptier. Lou's bed in the room the boys shared had not been slept in. His big wooden trunk was missing. His best jacket and all his shirts and the two pairs of boots—one for summer, one for winter—were missing from the wardrobe.

Wolf knew from the empty feeling under his breastbone that Lou was truly gone.

The only question he asked was "Where, Mama, where?"

Mama rushed out of the room, her apron up over her head.

*

Tata called the children into the parlor, the one with the family pictures on the shelf, the one the children were not allowed in except for weddings or funerals or after the fasting on Yom Kippur.

Wolf went in and sat on the bench between Simcha and baby Aron. He tried to listen and yet not to listen because what he really wanted to hear was that Lou had only been *borrowed* for a few days, not gone. He heard in his mind the rabbi saying *pilpul.*

"Your brother Lyovka," Tata began in the formal voice he saved for punishments and toasts

14

at the seder, "is gone." He did not look at the children, but stared at the pictures on the shelf. He touched a picture of his own father with his stained finger, straightening it.

No one spoke.

"He has gone away to a school in Kiev taught by army officers."

The girls caught their breaths simultaneously. Wolf knew why. Jewish boys simply did not go to army schools. They went to *cheders* taught by the rabbi. They went for further study at a *yeshiva*. But to go to an army school was unthinkable. There would be no kosher food. There would be work and study on the Sabbath. There would be fighting. It was not possible, yet—Wolf thought—if Tata says it is so, it is so.

"He will learn to march in an orderly fashion," Tata continued, "and to go in a straight line. He will learn to do as he is told and to keep the buttons on his uniform shining bright."

"He will hate that," said Wolf.

"What did you say?" Tata's voice held a terrible warning.

"Nothing, Tata." Wolf looked down, but he knew Tata had heard.

Standing by the window, Mama stared out at the gray sky. She did not say a word, but she sighed deeply. Wolf hated the sound of that sigh.

*

The first week Lou was gone he sent a letter to Mama and Tata complaining about the food. "All I can eat," he said, "are hard-boiled eggs. Nothing else is kosher." He sent a little note along to Wolf, reminding him he could play with the tin soldiers. "But only with great care."

The second week Lou sent a letter to Mama alone, with red ribbons enclosed for the girls.

The third week he sent a letter to Tata asking for money. Tata was angry, but still he sent some.

The fourth week there was no letter at all.

Autumn passed into winter. The leaves

17

swirled down from the trees, filling the soldiers' trenches and covering the village square. And still no more letters came from Lou.

In the kitchen Mama hardly spoke. On Fridays she pounded the *challah* dough with extra vehemence and braided it silently. Often she wiped tears from her eyes. The borscht she made was thin and watery. "As if she has cried into it," Wolf said to the girls.

Tata often stood by the window, smoking solemnly and gazing to the east, where Kiev lay.

The girls grew quiet like so many ghosts. Simcha grew loud and bossier than ever. Baby Aron learned all the verses of "Raisins and Almonds," which he proceeded to sing endlessly until Wolf shouted at him to stop. That made the two of them cry, Aron for being shouted at and Wolf, shocked, because he had shouted.

Then the snow fell. Wolf went outside alone. He walked along the soldiers' trenches pretending he had just rescued the lambs before one broke its leg. And he pretended further that he

returned each one to the proper farmer with no one the wiser.

He made one set of footprints near the oak tree, then another right beside it, so he could imagine that Lou was still there.

Then he went into the house and lined up the tin soldiers in a row. He made the general tell them all: "Lyovka is the bravest soldier we have. And for his bravery he shall be named the first Jewish general because he saved so many good men." He made a special medal shaped like a Jewish star cut from the bottom of the note Lou had sent and threaded it with a piece of ribbon he borrowed from one of his sisters.

But he could not tell Mama Lou's funny stories, no matter how hard he tried.

*

One day a letter came from the school in Kiev, delivered by Mischa the milkman. Wolf happened to be in the kitchen and took it, sniffing it as if some trace of Lou still lingered on the envelope. He ran right to the parlor where Tata

sat reading and Mama was stitching flowers onto a pillowcase.

"Look, Mama! Tata, look! A letter from the school. From Lou."

Tata did not even scold Wolf for coming into the parlor. He took the letter and set it on the table. Then he rose and poured himself a cup of tea from the steaming samovar.

"Aren't you going to open it, Tata?" Wolf asked.

Mama had put down her sewing. "Yes, Tata, read it," she said.

Tata opened the envelope, took out the piece of paper, and shook it till it unfolded. Then he reached into his vest pocket for his spectacles and began to read.

"Dear Mr. Yolen . . ." Tata stopped.

"It is not from Lou?" Mama asked, putting her hand over her heart.

Tata's eyes narrowed, and Wolf held his breath. Tata looked down and began reading again.

"Dear Mr. Yolen. Your son Lyovka was apprehended in an illegal card game. It was his third offense. This time he had gambled away all the gold buttons on his uniform. We had to send him home. It has been well over a month, and we are still awaiting instructions from him as to the disposition of his trunk. Signed: Vladimir Gospirin, Major General."

"Over a month?" Wolf whispered.

"Over a month?" Mama said aloud.

"Over a month?" came an echo from the doorway where the other children were peeking in.

"Then where is he?" Mama asked. "Where is Lou?"

Tata did not answer but crumpled up the letter and threw it into the stove where it burned with a sudden and angry flame.

The trunk came home at last but Lou did not. And if the house had been quiet before, now it was silent as a tomb. Mama hung cloths over each of the mirrors as a sign of mourning. When the girls wanted to comb their hair, they stationed Wolf at the door to warn of Mama's coming so they could peek into the mirror.

Wolf put the tin soldiers on the table in the boys' bedroom but would not play with them again. Still, he wouldn't give either Aron or Simcha permission to touch them. "Only Lou can do that," he said. He turned the general facedown.

Winter passed into spring, but no blossoms as yet had burst into color by the front door. The roads were muddy, but the soldiers' trenches

25

were still frozen solid. Playing in them was dangerous. A fall was like landing on iron. Even Simcha stayed indoors.

But Wolf went out. The house had become a kind of prison. Everywhere he could see Lou's things: the tin soldiers, the trunk, the bed were all reminders. And so he slipped outside, his scarf wound carefully around his neck and over his mouth.

Without meaning to, he found himself at the foot of the oak tree. Twice he turned away, angry with himself and angry with Lou for not being there. But the third time he thought: "What if the greenfinch has returned to the nest?"

With his mittens on, the climb was not easy and he only got a little way up the tree. Then he slipped down, one mitten riding up so that he scraped his palm badly, and he tore a piece out of his stocking as well.

When he got back home, he told no one of the accident, but soaked his hand in the brass basin until the scrape was clean. The torn stocking he hid in Lou's trunk.

The next day he went out again and this time he got more than halfway up. The third day he tore his other stocking and put it next to the first in the trunk. By the end of the week he could climb the tree with ease.

"If only *someone* could see me," he whispered when he got to the top. He meant Lou, but he wouldn't say the name aloud. He found the old nest and he tidied it up carefully. Then he sat staring for a long time down the road toward the east.

That night he set the tin general back up on the table, though he made sure its face was turned toward the wall.

*

For two weeks Wolf climbed the tree, settling himself in a crook, with his back against the strong trunk. He told himself stories out loud, stories that Lou had told. And then he began to tell some of his own. He practiced the stories,

polishing the phrases, building up to the last line.

"And then," he would say, "the rabbi said *pilpul*, but his eyes danced when he said it."

"And ever after," he said, "the Russian army named Jewish generals after the brave soldier Lou."

"And if you believe me," he whispered, "you will have caviar for breakfast and . . ." But his eyes got all hot and watery when he told himself this particular ending, so he did not finish.

*

One day Wolf was settling in the tree, his back against the scratchy bark, when he realized the leaves had begun to unfold all around him. Soon they would obscure his view of the road. There was a smell of real spring in the air, a promise of something strong and new pushing its way up from the south.

Wolf smiled. It was his first real smile in months. "The family *will* be happy once more," he said aloud, and he made himself look away from the road.

When he looked back, there a long way off
was a strange moving line. "Almost," he whispered, "a parade."

"The soldiers!" he shouted. He knew they
came back every spring to practice their marching and maneuvers in the trenches. Tata did not
like them. He said they drank too much and on
the Sabbath, too. Mama said they were much too
noisy. But Simcha would be pleased and would

make Wolf practice marching. And the girls would all find reasons to walk up and down outside the house.

He sank back against the tree. "No, it is too soon," he said aloud, meaning the soldiers only came when the mud was gone and the flowers were blooming, when all danger of snow was past. He wondered if, perhaps, he had *wanted* to see something coming down that road.

Leaning forward, Wolf stared as hard as he could and this time he realized that was not a line of soldiers he was seeing. For one thing, they were much too raggedy. For another, they were not in step. And for a third: "No guns!" he shouted. The soldiers always carried guns.

Suddenly the last figure in the line leaped up and fell over backwards, its feet wagging in the air like some sort of strange semaphore. The second to last and the third to last did the same. Wolf rubbed his eyes. What a strange thing! When he looked again all were upright as if nothing had happened.

Wolf stared, waiting for another such movement, but the line of men came closer and closer. And then—he nearly fell out of the tree in surprise. Shinnying down quickly, heedless of the scrape on his leg or that he had torn another stocking, Wolf jumped the last three feet to the ground. He ran back to the house, right into the parlor without even knocking.

"Mama!" he began. "Tata . . ."

Tata woke up from his nap, thunder on his face. "Look, indeed! Look at your shoes. Look at your stocking. And this is the Sabbath, too. Velvul, you are a disgrace." His voice was very quiet, which was even worse than when he shouted.

"But, look!" Wolf cried. "Look out the window. See who has come home."

Mama rose, even before Tata, and put her hand to her forehead. Wolf could see tears in her eyes. When he turned to his father, he was shocked to see there were tears in Tata's eyes as well.

"It is Lou!" cried Wolf, though they knew it already. "But who is it he has brought with him?"

4

They went to the door and stared: Mama and Tata and the girls and Aron clutching Tata's knees, and Simcha standing a bit to one side, hands on his hips, his face angry, as if preparing to say, "Go away, I am the oldest now. We do not need you."

Wolf stood in front, his mouth agape.

Coming toward them was Lou in an odd blue coat that fell loosely almost to his knees. His face was bony and his hair ragged and tied back with a string.

Behind him was a line of men, twelve in all. Each was the color of the new moon, though Lou was as white as the old one. The twelve men had eyes slanted like the mayor's cat, and black hair

skinned back into a long single braid. Wolf had
never seen anyone like them.

"Lou!" the girls called out together.

Lou looked up and waved. Mama put her

hand up over her eyes. Aron began to toddle down the road. But at a signal from Lou the twelve men moved out of line and Aron stopped still.

The first two men began to turn cartwheels, going so fast their feet became blurs. Three more began to flip forward, and three backwards.

Aron laughed and tried to do the same, falling over in a fit of giggles. Wolf went over and picked him up, dusting him off. The girls began to clap their hands. Even Tata smiled.

At another signal from Lou, the remaining four men lined up and then two of them held hands while the third climbed up onto their shoulders. He threw himself backwards into the air and, like a cat, landed on the shoulders of a fourth.

"Stop! Stop!" cried Mama. "Let me catch my breath, you rascal!"

But the men kept leaping and twisting and flying through the air until everyone was quite dizzy with watching.

Lou left the men, came over to Mama, and held her hands in his. "I could not come home to you in shame, Mama," he said. But his eyes twinkled as if to say: *So I came home in triumph.*

"No shame, no shame, my son, to come home," Mama said.

Tata's lips were pursed as if he had just sucked a lemon before drinking his tea. "And what is this you have brought with you?"

"After my little . . . problem in the school," Lou said, "I ran off to Moscow. There, I thought, I could prove myself. There, I thought, I could

win back your respect. I found work with a circus."

"What kind of work for a boy like you?" Tata asked.

"There is always work in a circus," said Lou. "There are animals to be fed and cages to be washed and money to be counted."

"And . . ." Tata did not say more, but his head inclined toward the men in the blue coats who were now standing as still as still.

"And now I am the manager of this fine team of Chinese acrobats," Lou said, gesturing to them with a grand sweep of his arm.

Tata's cheeks grew red and Mama's eyes shone with tears. Aron said "Ac-ro-bat, ac-ro-bat" over and over until Simcha shouted at him.

But Wolf did not say a word. Instead he went over to Lou and punched him as hard as he could, right in the stomach.

"*Oooof!*" said Lou, and he grabbed up Wolf, holding him close. "Is that any way to greet your brother who has been gone so long?"

Wolf struggled and shouted. "You did not write. Mama and the girls wept. Tata never smiled. Simcha was unbearable. And I never played with the tin soldiers, though they are braver than you ever were."

Lou was so surprised at this outburst, he dropped Wolf to the ground and turned to Mama and Tata. "What could I write when all was so bad? And isn't coming home as a manager of such a fine troop of acrobats a wonderful surprise?"

Tata looked grim. "They may be fine acrobats, but you may not be such a fine manager. I can see they have not been fed for many days. I suspect you have eaten little, too. There is probably still snow on some of the roads, and no one has extra food to give."

"Not eaten?" said Mama, wiping her eyes with a handkerchief.

"I promised them," Lou said, picking up Mama's hands once more, "I promised them my mama would feed them. I told them my tata would find them work."

Tata raised his finger to scold, but before he could, Mama opened the front door wide. "Come in, come in," she said to the acrobats. "Where there's love, there's room."

The twelve Chinese acrobats came in, one after another, bowing low to Mama and kissing her hand. But Wolf did not go into the house. Instead he walked off down the road to the oak tree and began the long climb.

This time he noticed how strong he had become, hardly hesitating about where to put his hands or feet. The tree limbs were familiar and comfortable beneath him.

When he got to the greenfinch nest, there was a feather in it, a winter feather, just shed.

"They are back," he whispered, and drew away, not wanting to frighten them.

He leaned against the trunk and tried to imagine Lou running away in shame. In his mind's eye

he saw the other students laughing and pointing their fingers at Lou. He saw Lou, without money or friends, walking the long road to Moscow. He saw him beg for work with the circus, cleaning the wild animal cages, and brushing the fur of the dancing bears until the little sparks came. He saw him greet the acrobats for the first time, bowing as low to them as they had bowed over Mama's hand.

He sighed and made himself fit perfectly against a little niche in the trunk, whispering, "And then Lou said: 'If you allow me to manage you, I will make you the toast of Moscow. You will have caviar for breakfast and . . .'"

"And champagne at each day's end." At the tree's foot stood Lou. He had washed the dirt of the road off his face but was still wearing the blue

Chinese jacket and his hair was still long and pulled back with its straggly string.

Wolf tried to look away, but Lou climbed up and sat next to him on a sturdy limb. It was difficult to ignore him when he was that close.

"You smell," Wolf said.

"I have been many days in these clothes," Lou said, "trying to get home."

"You could have written."

"I could not buy paper or ink. I needed my money for food."

They were silent for a long time. At last Lou said, "I am not good at studying, little brother. I am not happy being confined in one place. But I *can* make people happy. I *can* make them laugh. And I *can* manage a troop of Chinese acrobats."

"Manage to get them home at least," said Wolf. He allowed himself to lean just a little against Lou.

"So let me tell you about my adventures," said Lou.

"And I," said Wolf, "will tell you about mine."

*

Of course that is not the end of the story. Not entirely. The Chinese acrobats stayed the rest of the winter, working hard for Tata and eating Mama's good food. They kept the Sabbath and even went to synagogue, though they only learned a few of the Hebrew prayers. They taught the girls words in Chinese and baby Aron a Chinese game that went: "Gee lee, gu lu, turn the cake; add some oil, the better to bake. Gee lee, gu lu, now it's done; give a piece to every-one." Aron tried to play it with anyone who would listen. They showed Simcha how to turn somersaults and how to do running flips, until he tried one inside the house and broke Mama's favorite bowl.

They told Wolf many stories about their lives and Wolf memorized them all. They were wonderful tales, true tales, about a world so different from Wolf's cozy little village, his mind had to bend and stretch like an acrobat in order to accommodate them. Each night he wrote the stories down in a little notebook Lou gave him.

In late spring the acrobats went back to Moscow, looking for a circus. They carried baskets packed with *challah* and cheese and onions and flasks of water, for Mama would not let them leave without.

But Lou did not go with them. Tata sent him off to America. "Find us a place to stay," Tata said. "If you can manage a troop of Chinese acrobats on the road between Moscow and here, a troop of Yolens should be no trouble at all."

That is how Wolf grew up an American. He became a newspaperman, which is a kind of storyteller who likes true stories. When he married and had two children, we both became storytellers, too.

At least, that is how the family tells it.

There is plenty of room in stories for the truth—and other things. And in this story, plenty of room for love as well.